THE GRAIL, THE SHROUD,
& OTHER RELIGIOUS RELICS
Secrets & Ancient Mysteries

RELIGION & MODERN CULTURE
Title List

THE GRAIL, THE SHROUD, & OTHER RELIGIOUS RELICS
Secrets & Ancient Mysteries

by Kenneth McIntosh, M.Div.

Mason Crest Publishers
Philadelphia

Mason Crest Publishers Inc.
370 Reed Road
Broomall, Pennsylvania 19008
(866) MCP-BOOK (toll free)

First printing
1 2 3 4 5 6 7 8 9 10

Library of Congress Cataloging-in-Publication Data

McIntosh, Kenneth, 1959–
  The Grail, the Shroud & other religious relics : secrets & ancient mysteries / by Kenneth R. McIntosh.
      p. cm. — (Religion and modern culture)
  Includes index.
  ISBN 1-59084-978-7   ISBN 1-59084-970-1 (series)
  1. Relics--Juvenile literature. 2. Grail—Juvenile literature. I. Title. II. Series.
  BV890.M35 2006
  270—dc22

                                      2005013613

Produced by Harding House Publishing Service, Inc.
www.hardinghousepages.com
Interior design by Dianne Hodack.
Cover design by MK Bassett-Harvey.
Printed in India.

CONTENTS

INTRODUCTION

by Dr. Marcus J. Borg

You are about to begin an important and exciting experience: the study of modern religion. Knowing about religion—and religions—is vital for understanding our neighbors, whether they live down the street or across the globe.

Despite the modern trend toward religious doubt, most of the world's population continues to be religious. Of the approximately six billion people alive today, around two billion are Christians, one billion are Muslims, 800 million are Hindus, and 400 million are Buddhists. Smaller numbers are Sikhs, Shinto, Confucian, Taoist, Jewish, and indigenous religions.

Religion plays an especially important role in North America. The United States is the most religious country in the Western world: about 80 percent of Americans say that religion is "important" or "very important" to them. Around 95 percent say they believe in God. These figures are very different in Europe, where the percentages are much smaller. Canada is "in between": the figures are lower than for the United States, but significantly higher than in Europe. In Canada, 68 percent of citizens say religion is of "high importance," and 81 percent believe in God or a higher being.

The United States is largely Christian. Around 80 percent describe themselves as Christian. In Canada, professing Christians are 77 percent of the population. But religious diversity is growing. According to Harvard scholar Diana Eck's recent book *A New Religious America*, the United States has recently become the most religiously diverse country in the world. Canada is also a country of great religious variety.

Fifty years ago, religious diversity in the United States meant Protestants, Catholics, and Jews, but since the 1960s, immigration from Asia, the Middle East, and Africa has dramatically increased the number of people practicing other religions. There are now about six million Muslims, four million Buddhists, and a million Hindus in the United States. To compare these figures to two historically important Protestant denominations in the United States, about 3.5 million are Presbyterians and 2.5 million are Episcopalians. There are more Buddhists in the United States than either of these denominations, and as many Muslims as the two denominations combined. This means that knowing about other religions is not just knowing about people in other parts of the world—but about knowing people in our schools, workplaces, and neighborhoods.

Moreover, religious diversity does not simply exist between religions. It is found within Christianity itself:

- There are many different forms of Christian worship. They range from Quaker silence to contemporary worship with rock music to traditional liturgical worship among Catholics and Episcopalians to Pentecostal enthusiasm and speaking in tongues.

- Christians are divided about the importance of an afterlife. For some, the next life—a paradise beyond death—is their primary motive for being Christian. For other Christians, the afterlife does not matter nearly as much. Instead, a relationship with God that transforms our lives this side of death is the primary motive.
- Christians are divided about the Bible. Some are biblical literalists who believe that the Bible is to be interpreted literally and factually as the inerrant revelation of God, true in every respect and true for all time. Other Christians understand the Bible more symbolically as the witness of two ancient communities—biblical Israel and early Christianity—to their life with God.

Christians are also divided about the role of religion in public life. Some understand "separation of church and state" to mean "separation of religion and politics." Other Christians seek to bring Christian values into public life. Some (commonly called "the Christian Right") are concerned with public policy issues such as abortion, prayer in schools, marriage as only heterosexual, and pornography. Still other Christians name the central public policy issues as American imperialism, war, economic injustice, racism, health care, and so forth. For the first group, values are primarily concerned with individual behavior. For the second group, values are also concerned with group behavior and social systems. The study of religion in North America involves not only becoming aware of other religions but also becoming aware of differences within Christianity itself. Such study can help us to understand people with different convictions and practices.

And there is one more reason why such study is important and exciting: religions deal with the largest questions of life. These questions are intellectual, moral, and personal. Most centrally, they are:

- What is real? The religions of the world agree that "the real" is more than the space-time world of matter and energy.
- How then shall we live?
- How can we be "in touch" with "the real"? How can we connect with it and become more deeply centered in it?

This series will put you in touch with other ways of seeing reality and how to live.

Chapter 1

RELIGION & MODERN CULTURE

RELICS—AN ENDLESS FASCINATION

Robert Langdon is running for his life. The police have falsely accused him of murder, and he is fleeing from the police and a fanatical assassin. In the company of a beautiful stranger, Sophie Noveu, this Harvard professor finds himself in the midst of a deadly adventure. Together, Langdon and Noveu escape from the fortress-like security of the Louvre Museum, gain access to a secret Swiss bank vault, and acquire a mysterious object. They arrive at the home of Langdon's friend Leigh Teabing, an authority on the **Holy Grail**; the Grail is at the heart of this mystery, and in his lap, Teabing holds a wooden box that, when unlocked, will begin to reveal the Holy Grail's secrets.

The Holy Grail

These fictional events take place in the first half of *The Da Vinci Code*, a runaway best seller by Dan Brown. A former English teacher, Brown combined **conspiracy theories**, **New Age** religion, and an appreciation for art to create his novel. *The Da Vinci Code* has sold more than seven million copies. The hardcover edition has generated over $210 million in sales.

The Da Vinci Code is the latest link in an ancient chain—the myth of the Holy Grail. This myth, in turn, is only a building block of a larger phenomenon: the **Western** world's fascination with sacred relics. For at least two thousand years, holy objects have intrigued the religious and skeptical alike. In the twenty-first century, interest has not abated.

Indiana Jones, for example, is one of the most popular film heroes of the past twenty-five years. The first movie about him, *Raiders of the Lost Ark*, concerned the Ark of the Covenant. The third Indiana Jones movie, *The Last Crusade*, involved the Holy Grail. Furthermore, the popular *Tomb Raider* films, in which lovely Lara Croft dazzles her way through archeological treasure troves, also focus on ancient spiritual relics, while the 2005 film *Constantine* revolves around the **Spear of Destiny**.

RELICS IN THE SCRIPTURES

The word "relic" in its general sense simply means "an antiquity that has survived from the distant past." A boy who finds an Indian arrowhead in a field may say he has found a "relic." A vintage Volkswagen might be referred to as a relic from the sixties. However, the meaning of the word in this book is more precise. A sacred relic is, "a part of the body or object that belonged to a saint or holy person." Such objects are valued because they bolster religious faith, or because they are the alleged cause of miracles.

The Bible contains accounts of sacred relics; for example, Hebrew scripture (what Christians refer to as the Old Testament) tells the story

GLOSSARY

agnostics: Those who believe it is impossible to know whether or not God exists.

conspiracy theories: Ideas that others are plotting to commit an illegal or subversive act.

Coptic: Relating to the Copts, a people descended from the ancient Egyptians.

Crusaders: Those involved in the military expeditions made by European Christians from the eleventh to the thirteenth centuries to retake areas captured by Muslims.

evangelicals: People belonging to any Protestant church whose members believe in the authority of the Bible and salvation through personal acceptance of Jesus Christ.

Holy Grail: According to legend, the cup used by Jesus at the Last Supper and by Joseph of Arimathea to collect Jesus's blood and sweat at the Crucifixion.

medieval: Relating to or typical of the Middle Ages in Europe.

New Age: A movement dating from the 1980s that emphasizes spiritual consciousness, and often belief in reincarnation and astrology and the practice of meditation, vegetarianism, and holistic medicine.

Pagans: People whose religion does not follow one of the world's main religions, especially those who are not Christian, Jewish, or Muslim, and whose religion is sometimes regarded as questionable.

Spear of Destiny: According to legend, the lance that was thrust into Jesus's side to see if he was dead, and that can bring its bearer world control.

theologians: Experts in the study of religion and God's relationship to the world.

Western: Found in or typical of countries, especially in Europe and North and South America, whose culture and society are influenced primarily by Greek and Roman traditions and Christianity.

Wiccans: People involved in the practice of Wicca, an ancient Pagan religion involving nature-worship.

"The legend of the Grail, more than any other western myth, has retained the vital magic which marks it as a living legend capable of touching both imagination and spirit. No other myth is so rich in symbolism, so diverse and often contradictory in its meaning."

—*Malcolm Godwin, author of* The Holy Grail: Its Origins, Secrets & Meaning Revealed

of Elisha's miraculous bones in 2 Kings, chapter 13, where gravediggers throw another man's body into Elisha's grave. "As soon as the man touched the bones of Elisha he revived and stood on his feet." From this account, teachers in the early Christian church concluded that the Holy Spirit inhabits the bones of especially holy men and women, even after their death. According to ancient Christian tradition, this Spirit in the saints' remains works miracles.

The Christian New Testament offers another account of miracle-working relics. The book of Acts, chapter 19 reveals, "God did extraordinary miracles by the hand of Paul, so that handkerchiefs or aprons were carried away from his body to the sick, and diseases left them and evil spirits came out of them." Based on this account, **theologians** expanded their beliefs regarding relics. Not only could the bodies of saints wield miracles, but even objects touched by the saints carried supernatural power.

Faith in relics' miraculous powers continues today. When a young man suffered from cancer, for example, a nun gave him a special gift: a crucifix touched by Saint Padre Pio. The kindhearted woman believed it held healing power because a holy man had handled it.

The Da Vinci Code is likely to become even bigger in May of 2006 with the release of the movie version. Ron Howard, director of award-winning movies *The Missing* and *A Beautiful Mind*, will direct the film. Tom Hanks, one of the United States' most popular actors, will star as Robert Langdon.

RELICS IN HISTORY

The first Christians held onto objects associated with their friends and loved ones after death, just as many people do today. Early Christians especially valued objects associated with martyrs, those who had suffered and died for their faith.

Over the next two centuries, Christians attached increasingly greater value to martyrs' relics. They believed the martyrs, because of their willingness to suffer for God, gained special favor with God. By touching a martyr's relic, a believer on earth could experience a special connection with the spirit of the martyr. Doing so, she could expect a miracle.

The Catholic Church decreed in 386 CE that saints' relics could not be bought or sold. This was an attempt to remove the blessings of God from crass moneymaking. However, people still used relics to make money in other ways. For instance, if a church possessed an especially powerful relic, pilgrims would travel far to see it, and these pilgrims would need to rent rooms at inns and buy meals . . . and they donated

money to the church where the relic was kept. Obviously, owning relics gave churches an economic advantage.

By the Middle Ages, saints' relics were hugely popular. Churches, castles, and towns became famous by merit of the relics they possessed. Pilgrims would travel for weeks, months, and sometimes even years to touch religious relics. Victims of disease sought healing primarily by means of miraculous cures via relics. Relics dominate the great myths of the *medieval* world, such as that of King Arthur.

In the year 1510, a young monk journeyed to Rome. He visited the various relics but was not impressed. As many young people do, he was forming his own beliefs about God and the Church. He believed each Christian should approach God directly, rather than travel and pay money to see relics. His name was Martin Luther, and a few years later, his actions would forever divide the Christian church. According to Luther, faith in Jesus Christ alone held the power to work miracles. Relics were unnecessary.

Prince Frederick the Wise, who ruled Saxony where Luther lived, owned more than five thousand sacred objects. His collection included a piece of baby Jesus's diaper, straw from the Holy Manger, a hair from Jesus's beard, one of the nails that held Jesus on the cross, and a piece of bread from the Last Supper. Annually, Frederick allowed pilgrims to see these relics. This was a big moneymaking event for the Kingdom of Saxony. Yet the upstart monk, Luther, prevailed: Frederick gave up his collection.

Today, Protestants are Christians who follow Luther's main ideas. Most Protestant churches do not display the bones of saints. Roman Catholic, Orthodox, and *Coptic* churches, however, continue to embrace the power of the spirit allegedly contained within sacred relics. These traditions are a precious part of the faith of many Christians today.

However, interest in relics in the twenty-first century cuts across religious barriers. The Shroud of Turin, owned by the Catholic Church, fascinates *evangelicals*, spiritual seekers, and even *agnostics*. The Holy

"The Holy Grail is a symbol, a metaphor and an idea that sprang from the fertile imagination of medieval storytellers. You will find it digging in books, legends and myths, but not in the ground."

—*biblical archaeologist Ben Witherington III*

Grail tantalizes New Agers, **Pagans**, and **Wiccans**—as well as Christians. Relics continue to fascinate people of all sorts—perhaps because they hold the power of myth.

RELICS & MYTH

A Roman Catholic Web site offers the following definition of myth:

> An imaginative story using symbols and colorful images to help us understand a truth either too complicated or too difficult to express in words. Unfortunately, most modern readers consider *myth* to be equivalent to *fairy tale*—a good story perhaps but without truth. This understanding of myth, however, is very different from what the sacred writer and biblical scholar would intend. A myth is a human way of exploring and dealing with a mysterious truth.

Some social scientists suggest that everyone believes myths of some sort. It does not matter if one is religious or atheist, communist or cap-

DATING SYSTEMS & THEIR MEANING

You might be accustomed to seeing dates expressed with the abbreviations BC or AD, as in the year 1000 BC or the year AD 1900. For centuries, this dating system has been the most common in the Western world. However, since BC and AD are based on Christianity (BC stands for Before Christ and AD stands for *anno Domini*, Latin for "in the year of our Lord"), many people now prefer to use abbreviations that people from all religions can be comfortable using. The abbreviations BCE (meaning Before Common Era) and CE (meaning Common Era) mark time in the same way (for example, 1000 BC is the same year as 1000 BCE, and AD 1900 is the same year as 1900 CE), but BCE and CE do not have the same religious overtones as BC and AD.

italist. According to this view, science, history, psychology, and religion all provide myths. We all buy into grand stories of one sort or another that tell us who we are and how the world works.

Relics are objects associated with stories that provide spiritual truth. Stories of the Holy Grail are especially rich in mythic symbolism. Indeed, there are at least a hundred different myths attached to this ancient concept.

Many books on the Grail and the Shroud contain numerous inaccuracies. Some authors have falsified history in order to make new and provocative claims, thus selling more books. This book is concerned with historical accuracy. Nevertheless, it is sometimes impossible to say where history ends and fantasy starts.

Concerning holy relics, the public always wants to know, "Is it real?" Historians tell us that most sacred relics are not the actual objects they are alleged to be. Because a great demand for relics existed in the Middle Ages, numerous relics were manufactured during that time. Others may indeed be ancient, but there is no possible way to prove they are the actual sacred objects.

At the same time, worshippers have regarded the relics discussed in this book as sacred objects over the centuries. Whether they date to medieval times or Bible times, they are nonetheless treasures.

In Saint Catherine's Monastery in the Sinai Desert, for example, grows the plant claimed to be Moses's burning bush. Even if Saint Catherine's Monastery is on the actual Mount Sinai where Moses heard God's voice (archaeologists debate that), and even if the bush is a very rare species (naturalists say it is), how can anyone prove it is the bush from which God spoke to Moses? However, it is very old. It is likely the same bush pilgrims have journeyed to see for more than 1,500 years. From ancient times, travelers have come to Saint Catherine's Monastery and prayed before this bush. Saint Helena, the mother of Constantine the Great, saw the bush in the fourth century and ordered construction of the monastery. Mohammed sent a letter to the monks promising Islam would guard their habitation. *Crusaders* wept and knelt before the bush, after fighting halfway around the world. It may or may not be Moses's bush, but it is a powerful relic.

THE RELICS OF THE VATICAN

By the beginning of the sixteenth century, the Vatican housed a huge collection of saints' relics. In the crypt of St. Callistus alone, forty popes and 76,000 martyrs were buried. Relics that Rome claimed included a piece of the burning bush through which God spoke to Moses, the portrait of Christ on the napkin of Veronica, and the bodies of St. Peter and St. Paul.

Some relics are famous not for their existence, but for their absence. Most archaeologists believe the Ark of the Covenant really existed in the time of King David, three thousand years ago. The ancient Jews believed the awesome presence of God inhabited the ark. However, it disappeared around the time of Christ. Steven Spielberg and George Lucas made the ark famous again with their movie, *Raiders of the Lost Ark*. Since then people have wondered, "Where is the real ark?"

Chapter 2

THE LOST ARK OF THE COVENANT

RELIGION & MODERN CULTURE

Marcus Brody is an aging college professor who is helping his younger colleague, Indiana Jones, pack for an archaeological expedition. Indiana is wondering if an old girlfriend, Marion Ravenwood, will be willing to give him a clue that leads to the ark. Brody tells him, "Marion's the least of your worries right now, believe me, Indy."

Jones replies, "What do you mean?"

Marcus has a worried look on his face. "Well, I mean that for nearly three thousand years man has been searching for the lost ark. It's not something to be taken lightly. No one knows its secrets. It's like nothing you've ever gone after before."

RELIGION & MODERN CULTURE

"All your life has been spent in pursuit of archeological relics. Inside the Ark are treasures beyond your wildest aspirations. You want to see it opened as well as I. Indiana, we are simply passing through history. This, this is history."

—*Belloq, the villain of* Indiana Jones and the Raiders of the Lost Ark

Jones laughs at Brody's worries.

> Oh, Marcus. What are you trying to do, scare me? You sound like my mother. We've known each other for a long time. I don't believe in magic, a lot of superstitious hocus pocus. I'm going after a find of incredible historical significance, you're talking about the boogie man. Besides, you know what a cautious fellow I am.

As he finishes speaking, Jones throws a large revolver into his suitcase.

This scene takes place in the early part of a popular adventure movie, *Indiana Jones and the Raiders of the Lost Ark*, one of the most successful films of the 1980s. Fans of the film know that Marcus Brody had plenty of reason to worry. Indiana Jones has to battle sword-wielding assassins and machine-gun carrying Nazis. German soldiers throw Indy and Marion into a pit full of deadly snakes. After escaping from the pit, Jones risks life and limb chasing a German army truck on horseback. Finally, Jones and Ravenwood barely escape death as the wrath of God pours out of the ark, devouring an entire Nazi platoon. At the movie's end, the U.S. Army is hiding the ark "somewhere very safe."

Although it is fiction, *Raiders of the Lost Ark* introduced millions of movie fans to the Ark of the Covenant. In an early scene, government

THE LOST ARK OF THE COVENANT

25

officials ask Jones and Brody about a coded message they have intercepted from the German military. Indiana and Brody exclaim, "The Nazis are going after the Ark of the Covenant." The military officials are obviously puzzled, but Jones explains, "The Ark of the Covenant, the chest that the Hebrews used to carry around the Ten Commandments."

One of the government men asks, "What, you mean *the* Ten Commandments?"

Jones replies, "Yes, the actual Ten Commandments, the original stone tablets that Moses brought down from Mt. Ararat and smashed, if you believe in that sort of thing. . . ."

The government men stare at Jones blankly. They are obviously confused. Indy asks them, "Didn't any of you guys ever go to Sunday school?" The two officials stare at each other sheepishly.

Before the Indiana Jones movie—and even more after it—this ancient missing relic has fascinated archaeologists and history buffs. What was the Ark of the Covenant in the first place? What was its terrifying power? Where is it today?

THE ARK IN THE SCRIPTURES

The ark first appears in the book of Exodus in the Torah (the Torah is the first five books of the Hebrew scriptures). After giving Moses the Ten Commandments, God gives him detailed instructions regarding the ark: "They shall make an ark of acacia wood; two cubits and a half shall be its length, a cubit and a half its breadth, and a cubit and a half its height" (a biblical cubit is the length from an adult's elbow to the fingertips). God further commands the Israelites to cover this ark with gold. He tells them to fashion two cherubim (angels), facing each other, on top of the ark. God also instructs the Israelites to carry the ark by means of poles, fitted through rings on the side of the box, and forbids mortals to touch the ark for any reason. Then God promises his people, "I will speak to you" from the ark.

An artisan named Bez'alel fashions the ark exactly as God commanded. Shortly after that, the book of Numbers reports, "When Moses went into the tent of meeting to speak with the Lord, he heard the voice speaking to him from above the ark of the testimony, from between the two cherubim; and it spoke to him."

The ark's formidable reputation comes from incidents described in the later books of Joshua and 1 Samuel. After Moses dies, the Israelites set out to take possession of the Promised Land called Canaan. To enter Canaan, all the tribes of Israel must cross the river Jordan. Priests carrying the ark by its poles step into the river, and the waters miraculously part so they can walk across it. The Israelites march to the walled Canaanite city of Jericho. The priests carrying the ark walk in circles around the town, and its walls come crashing down. Later, in the book of 1 Samuel, the Philistines, Israel's enemies, capture the ark. The Philistines set the ark in the temple of their god, Dagon. As a result, the great statue of Dagon comes crashing to the temple floor. The Philistines move the ark to the city of Ashdod—and the citizens of Ashdod promptly become ill with tumors. The Philistines move the ark to the city of Gath, where the same thing happens. At this point, the Philistines return the ark to the Israelites.

WHAT IS THE ARK?

In recent years, several theories have emerged regarding the ark's extraordinary properties. Some people suggest it may have been an enormous battery—an amazing example of early technology. Others wonder if perhaps it came from outer space; maybe alien technology explains its unusual capabilities. Archaeologists and Bible scholars scoff at such ideas.

The Hebrew word translated "ark" means simply, "box, chest, container." The ancient Hebrews made it to hold something. As mentioned

A DANGEROUS OBJECT

The Second Book of Samuel records a deadly incident involving the ark when King David ordered the ark brought to Jerusalem. The people placed the ark on an oxcart, which was against God's orders. (He had commanded that people must always carry the ark by its poles.) As the oxcart bumped along, the ark began to slide off. A priest named Uzzah reached out to steady the ark. "And God smote him there because he put forth his hand to the ark: and he died there beside the Ark of God." The movie *Raiders of the Lost Ark* also portrays the dangerous nature of this sacred vessel. At the movie's end, the Nazis open the lid of the ark, and its horrifying power literally melts the German troops. In the Bible and in modern myth, those who possess the ark must treat it very carefully.

above, it held the Ten Commandments—but this alone does not explain its power. To understand the amazing stories about the ark's power, we must first ask, "What exactly is the ark?"

In recent years, archaeological discoveries in Egypt have added to archaeologists' understanding of the ark. The ancient Egyptians had a number of portable shrines. Two Egyptian metal plaques from the sixth

century BCE portray such a shrine for the god Amon-Re, amazingly similar to the description of the ark in Exodus. It is a box with a winged being facing the center of the top, with poles for carrying placed through rings on the side. Its dimensions are also similar to the biblical ark. The Egyptians used portable shrines to carry statues of their gods, and they treated these idols as the very presence of the gods themselves.

The ark is Israel's portable shrine. Archaeologists and Bible scholars recall that Moses grew up in Egypt; he and his fellow Israelites would have been familiar with Egyptian portable shrines. In the Torah, God forbids Israel from making idols. Thus, unlike Egyptian portable shrines, the ark did not contain an image of the Lord. Nonetheless, it likely had meaning for the Israelites similar to the meaning of the portable shrines for the Egyptians. The ark was a symbol of God's presence.

In Bible stories, the power of the ark is the power of the Lord. The Israelites believed God worked miracles on their behalf. By attaching his miracles to the presence of the ark, God made it clear he was doing these things for them.

WHEN DID THE ARK DISAPPEAR?

Catholic Bibles have several books not in the Protestant Bible, and one of these, 2 Maccabees, gives an account of the ark's disappearance. In 587 BCE, the Babylonian army destroyed Jerusalem and Solomon's Temple. That Temple was the home of the ark. Second Maccabees records that prior to the destruction of Jerusalem, God instructed the prophet Jeremiah to hide the ark. Jeremiah took the ark up Mount Nebo, which borders Israel in the nation of Jordan. "Jeremiah came and found a cave-dwelling, and he brought there the tent and the ark and the altar of incense; then he sealed up the entrance."

One might think this would settle the issue of the ark's whereabouts, at least for faithful Catholics, but there is a hitch. The book of 2 Maccabees records the finding of a document that tells this story of Jeremiah hiding the ark. According to Catholic theology, when the Bible quotes another document, the information contained therein may or may not be true. In other words, according to the Catholic Church, the Bible does not actually say where the ark is—it just gives a clue where it *might* be. There are other clues as to the ark's whereabouts.

The Revelation of Esdras is part of the Apocrypha—books that Jewish and Christian authorities refused to accept as part of the Bible, though the books claim to be divinely inspired. The Revelation of Esdras says that Nebuchadnezzar's invading army took the ark to Babylon after they conquered Jerusalem in 587 BCE.

An ancient Jewish tradition is also recorded in the Talmud, a collection of sayings by famous Jewish teachers. According to this tradition, secret tunnels lay underneath the Temple in Jerusalem, and when it became obvious that Roman armies were about to overtake the Holy City in 70 CE, priests hid the ark in these underground passageways.

Will we ever really know what happened to the lost ark? Joseph Pelligrino, a brilliant writer, scientist, and adventurer—sometimes called "the real Indiana Jones"—says, "The fate of the Ark, hidden or lost for all time, is one more archaeological mystery that, barring acts of God, I think will be successfully plumbed someday."

A completely different—and equally fascinating—tradition about the ark is recorded in Ethiopia, where Jewish people have lived for thousands of years. The Ethiopian Jews say they are descendants of King Solomon and the Queen of Sheba. Scripture tells how the Queen of Sheba came to visit Solomon and admired his wealth. According to Ethiopian tradition, the Queen of Sheba and Solomon exchanged more than compliments; they say the queen bore a son by Solomon. After he reached manhood, the other princes in Jerusalem rejected this half-Ethiopian son of the king. Disenchanted, he returned to Ethiopia—taking the Ark of the Covenant with him.

REAL-LIFE RAIDERS OF THE LOST ARK

As you might expect, archaeologists and amateur adventurers have sought the lost ark in all the places where they thought it could be located. Following the book of Maccabees, Catholic archaeologists have done extensive excavations on Mount Nebo. They have unearthed fabulous remains from the early Christian era and fascinating prehistoric remains, but no Ark of the Covenant.

Conservative Jews in Jerusalem tend to believe the account found in the Talmud. However, Islam now owns the site of Solomon's Temple. The mosque known as the Dome of the Rock sits atop the site where the ark sat in ancient times. Digging under the Dome of the Rock is forbidden.

In 1981, three rabbis claimed they had tunneled under the Dome of the Rock and discovered the secret passages. Two of them, Shlomo Goren and Yehuda Getz, say they actually saw the Ark of the Covenant in a hidden chamber. Rabbi Goren says, "Unfortunately, when we came too close, the Arabs started rioting and they would not let us return to the tunnels." Today, visitors to Jerusalem can take an underground tour from the Western Wall (also known as the Wailing Wall) toward the site of Solomon's Temple. Guides point to a tunnel, heading under the Dome of the Rock, which Arab workers have completely filled in to block any further exploration. Does the Ark of the Covenant lie on the other side of the blockage, as these rabbis claim?

Graham Hancock is not too interested in the tunnels underneath Jerusalem. Hancock, an English citizen and reporter of African news, is convinced the ark is in Axum, Ethiopia. Almost all Ethiopian Jews and Christians believe this. Hancock spent years attempting to see the ark, but Ethiopian priests guard it carefully, and he was unable to do so. Nonetheless, Hancock is convinced the ark is in Ethiopia.

Finally, members of the Masonic order of the Templars suspect the ark is on Scottish soil. After the conquest of Jerusalem by Crusaders in 1099, a group of warrior monks known as the Knights Templar built their headquarters on the Temple Mount. They dug for relics on the site, and although no actual record exists, members of this fraternal society say the Templars found the Ark of the Covenant. Centuries later, when the Catholic Church turned against the Templars and church authorities burned many Templar knights at the stake, King Robert the Bruce of Scotland protected the surviving members of the order. The art and architecture of Rosslyn Chapel in Scotland, an ornate church built

not long after Robert the Bruce died, bear the marks of the Knights' influence—and members of the Order of the Templars claim that Knights hid the ark in the chapel. Archaeologists and professional historians give little credence to this story, but the novel *The Da Vinci Code* has added to the fame of this theory.

The Ark of the Covenant is a mystery because it is lost. It remains the ultimate lost treasure. Other relics, however, have the opposite problem—too many people claim to possess them.

Throughout the centuries since the foundation of Christianity, one of the most famous—and most faked—artifacts is the Cross of Christ. Related to that are multiple artifacts claimed to be the Lance of Longinus, the spear that pierced Christ on the Cross. Some people even believe the spear holds the key to world supremacy!

Chapter 3

THE TRUE CROSS & THE SPEAR OF DESTINY

RELIGION & MODERN CULTURE

In September of 1912, a pair of young men stood in Vienna's Hofburg Museum, staring at a piece of ancient iron in a glass case. One of the men, Dr. Walter Stein, would fade from history unnoticed. The other man, however, would influence history more horribly than any mortal before or after him. That young man was Adolf Hitler.

The object in the case had various names—the Holy Lance, the Spear of Destiny, and the Lance of Longinus. Along with many others, Hitler believed the Holy Lance was the spear that pierced the side of Jesus Christ as he hung on the cross. Allegedly, Hitler said later:

I stood there quietly gazing upon it for several minutes quite oblivious to the scene around me . . . I felt as though I myself had held it before in some earlier century of history. That I myself had once claimed it as my *talisman* of power and held the destiny of the world in my hands.

This quote, from a 1973 book by historian Trevor Ravenscroft titled *The Spear of Destiny*, is dubious, historically. Ravenscroft was an **occult** practitioner, and some historians believe he may have altered facts to support his own beliefs. However, whether Hitler made the comment or not, his actions revealed his obsession with the Holy Lance.

Historians call the Holy Lance in the Hofburg Museum the Spear of Destiny. Legends claim that the possessor of the spear controls the world—and Hitler was determined to possess the lance. On March 12, 1938, Nazi Germany took control of Austria, and that same day, Hitler drove to the Hofburg Museum to visit the Holy Lance. In August of 1938, Hitler's National Socialist government passed a law stating Germany's legal right to possess the Holy Lance (*Helige Lanz*). On October 13, 1938, heavily armed German troops escorted the Holy Lance on a train trip from Vienna to Nuremberg. For much of World War II, the lance resided in St. Katherine's Church in Nuremburg, the spiritual heart of the Third Reich. Later, when Allied planes were bombing Germany, Hitler moved the Spear of Destiny to a secure underground bunker.

At 3:00 P.M., on April 30, 1945, U.S. troops took possession of the underground bunker. Thirty minutes later, Adolf Hitler committed suicide. Chalk it up to fate—or coincidence—but believers in the spear note how it passed from Hitler's possession just before his final defeat, another chapter in the myth of the Holy Lance.

GLOSSARY

occult: Relating to, involving, or typical of the supposed supernatural, magic, or witchcraft.

talisman: An object believed to give magical powers to the person who wears or carries it.

THE CROSS & THE LANCE IN SCRIPTURE

Crucifixion was one of the most awful forms of torture and death ever invented. Victims hung from the crossbeam by nails in their wrists, while their ankles, in a flexed position, were nailed to the upright post. Suspended like this, a person could not breathe, unless he pushed himself upright. When he did so, unimaginable pain shot through the nerves that had been pierced by the nails. Thus, victims of crucifixion were continuously suffering, either from the collapse of their lungs or from horrendous pain in their limbs.

The four New Testament Gospels recount the Crucifixion of Jesus of Nazareth. According to the Gospels of Matthew and of Mark, a Roman centurion (an officer commanding a hundred men) who stood beneath

the cross when Jesus died exclaimed, "Surely, this man was the Son of God!" Luke's Gospel also mentions the centurion, but in Luke he exclaims, "Surely, this man was innocent!" The Gospel of John does not mention the centurion, but John adds a detail not found in the other Gospels. According to John, the Jewish authorities asked the Roman soldiers to hasten the execution of Jesus and the two men crucified beside him since it was Friday, and the Jewish religious leaders did not want the Sabbath Day (Saturday) contaminated by death. The Romans observed that Jesus appeared to be dead, but to make sure, "one of the soldiers pierced his side with a spear, and at once there came out blood and water." The Gospels do not name the centurion or the soldier who pierced Christ's side with the spear.

THE MYTH OF LONGINUS

Three centuries after the Crucifixion of Jesus Christ, an anonymous author wrote *The Gospel of Nicodemus*. It was a popular work, and eventually translators rendered the book into every European language and hundreds of slightly differing versions. According to *The Gospel of Nicodemus*, the centurion who proclaimed Christ the Son of God is the same soldier who pierced Christ's side with the spear. *The Gospel of Nicodemus* gave this man a name—Gaius Cassius Longinus. The book also added more detail to the story: Longinus became blind sometime before the Crucifixion, and another man guided his hands to pierce Christ's side. When Jesus's blood flowed down the spear shaft, Longinus wiped his eyes with a hand covered by the blood—and at once, God healed his blindness. According to this story, this miracle was what led Longinus to confess, "This man was the Son of God."

"The Nazis have had teams of archaeologists running around the world looking for all kinds of religious artifacts. Hitler is a nut on the subject."

—*A U.S. government agent speaking with Indiana Jones, in the movie* Raiders of the Lost Ark

THE HOLY LANCE IN HISTORY

Over the long course of history, several different Holy Lances have appeared, each alleged to be *the* spear that pierced Christ on the cross.

In the year 326, Empress Helena, the mother of Emperor Constantine the Great, made a highly celebrated journey to the Holy Land. She spent her trip locating holy places and holy relics. Early reports of her journey tell of Helena finding the True Cross on which Christ was crucified. Later accounts say she found the cross, the crown of thorns, the post on which Christ was whipped, and the Holy Lance.

The lance known today as the Spear of Destiny first appears in the *History of Luitprand of Cremona*, which he completed in 961. Luitprand says nothing about it being the Lance of Longinus, but says the spear is "a treasure by which God binds the earthly and the celestial." A legend grew that whoever possessed the lance would be able to conquer the world. Napoleon attempted to obtain the lance after the battle of Austerlitz, but it had been smuggled out of the city before the battle started, and he never got hold of it. As described earlier, Hitler was a true believer in the legend of the spear and went to great efforts to attain and keep it.

The Holy Lance seemed to multiply, however—or at least stories of its discovery did. A century after the Spear of Destiny appeared in history, the Crusaders found another alleged Holy Lance.

THE LANCE, THE GRAIL, & KING ARTHUR

From *The Gospel of Nicodemus,* the story of Longinus passed into the later King Arthur legends. According to English tradition, Joseph of Arimathea brought the Lance of Longinus, along with the Holy Grail, to Britain soon after Christ's death. Longinus's spear, still miraculously wet with the blood of Christ, passed to a Christian king living in Britain, who was known as the Fisher King. The Fisher King had a castle that contained "the Grail Hallows," sacred relics associated with Christ that included the Holy Grail, the Holy Lance, and the platter with John the Baptist's head on it.

Sustained by these holy relics, the Fisher King was able to live for centuries. However, tragedy struck when the Holy Spear was stuck in his groin. Various reasons are given for this accident. One version says he lusted after a young woman; another says he lost his Christian faith; and yet another version involves a quarrel. Legends refer to the Fisher King's accident with the spear as the *Dolorous Stroke*. The *Dolorous Stroke* affected more than the Fisher King: all Britain became a wasteland, and animals, forests, and humans became sickly and unhappy. In order for the Wasteland to be restored to "merry old England," King Arthur's knights had to successfully undertake the quest for the Holy Grail.

The first Crusade was in a tight spot. The armies of Islam had the Europeans pinned down in Antioch, far north of Jerusalem, their intended destination. In the midst of this crisis, one of the Crusaders, Peter Bartholomew, had a dream, telling him to dig underneath St. Peter's Cathedral. He did so and found the Holy Lance. According to the story, this greatly encouraged the Crusaders and spurred them on to victory. Of course, not everyone was thrilled. The Germans who possessed the Spear of Destiny believed *they* held the real Holy Lance.

THE TRUE CROSS IN HISTORY

For the Roman soldiers, the cross that held Jesus of Nazareth was just one of many they had constructed. Grisly executions were regular business for these soldiers. They could never have guessed that their gruesome tool of death would become the world's most common religious symbol. (To catch a glimpse of how strange this symbol is, imagine if a noose, a guillotine, or an electric chair were transformed into an icon of faith.)

Throughout the centuries, Christians have felt great devotion to the cross. This devotion is based on New Testament accounts of Christ's death as a demonstration of God's love for humanity. According to Christian theology, Christ's agony on the cross acts as a bridge between God and human beings who are bent from the shape God intended for them; it offers eternal life to the entire world. Within decades of Christ's death, the Apostle Paul wrote to the church in Corinth about "Christ crucified . . . the power of God and the wisdom of God." The recent popular movie *The Passion of the Christ*, produced by Catholic filmmaker Mel Gibson, gives a sense of the importance of Christ's death to Christian believers.

Since the cross has such powerful symbolic meaning for Christians, it was inevitable that believers would desire to touch the actual, physical artifact. As stated earlier, the first mention of the cross being found is in 326 CE when the Empress Helena ordered it excavated in Jerusalem. Helena sent pieces of what she believed to be the True Cross to her son, Emperor Constantine. He placed the nails from the cross on his horse's bridle and his helmet, and went about conquering enemies, allegedly by the power of God.

After the initial discovery of the True Cross, it somehow seemed to proliferate, just as the Holy Lance had. Kings, churches, and wealthy merchants boasted their own piece of Christ's cross. According to medieval historians, if someone had combined all the pieces of the "True Cross" together, they would have formed a cross larger than the Eiffel Tower. Kings led their knights to war with splinters of the cross in golden caskets marching ahead of them, like the Ark of the Covenant going to war with the Israelites. Peasants and nobles alike attributed innumerable healings and miracles to fragments of the cross.

THE RELICS OF CHRIST'S PASSION TODAY

The Spear of Destiny is on display at the Kunsthistorisches Museum, Vienna. Tests performed on the metal have proven that a weapons maker forged the lance in medieval times, so it cannot be the actual lance of a first-century Roman centurion. The mystical power that Hitler and others attached to the Spear of Destiny existed only in their own convictions.

However, the Spear of Destiny demonstrates the power of myth to influence lives. Hitler and Napoleon believed the Holy Lance could control the destinies of their empires. Although it is not a genuine relic of the Crucifixion, it is a piece of history.

The alleged Holy Lance found by the Crusaders still exists today. That lance is kept in Armenia's Wonder Museum of Holy Echmiadzin.

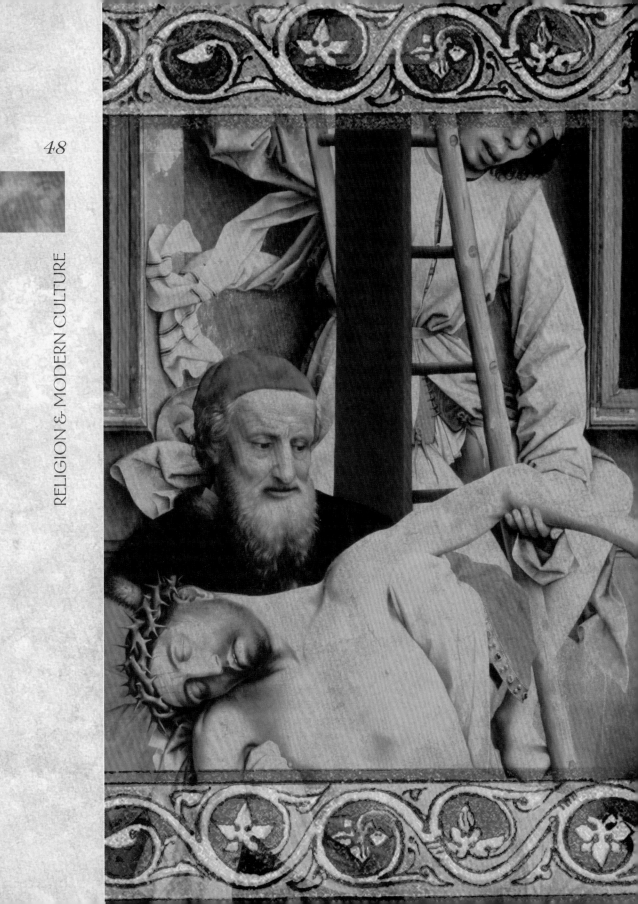

"On a hill far away stood an old rugged cross,
The emblem of suffering and shame;
And I love that old cross where the dearest and best,
For a world of lost sinners was slain."

—*opening line of the hymn, "The Old Rugged Cross," by George*
Bennard, 1913

Archaeologists say it is not actually a Roman lance but the head of a Roman standard.

The 2005 movie *Constantine*, which starred Keanu Reeves and Rachel Weisz, built its plot around the Spear of Destiny. In that movie, the spear is the tool that will enable Satan to overcome the forces of good in the world. The prop used for the spear in the film is a copy of the lance in Vienna.

As for the True Cross, portions are on display in various European churches, cathedrals, and museums. They are common enough that collectors sell them on eBay. A search of that Internet auction site done in January 2004 found a dozen True Cross relics for sale with prices ranging from $225 to $1,200.

Throughout the Middle Ages, the cross and associated relics were vital to the faith of most Christian believers. After the Middle Ages, interest in the True Cross waned. After World War II, the Spear of Destiny also faded in importance. The flood of forgeries caused most people to lose their faith in these alleged holy artifacts. However, in recent years another relic that was popular in the fourteenth century has become even more popular. The Shroud of Turin has unique and unexplainable properties that make it a subject of enduring fascination.

Chapter 4

THE SHROUD OF TURIN

RELIGION & MODERN CULTURE

The Shroud of Turin is a piece of cloth, approximately fourteen feet (4 meters) long and three feet (about 1 meter) wide. On the shroud is the faint yellowish image of a naked man, portrayed from the front and from the back, along with apparent spots of blood. The body was evidently tortured before death. Some Christians say this is the burial shroud of Jesus Christ.

As the nineteenth century neared its end, many intellectuals in Europe and North America believed science would soon disprove religion. In the year 1898, however, the new science of photography unleashed a wave of interest in a religious artifact, the Shroud of Turin. That wave of interest has not slowed.

In 1898, the shroud was popular only in its native city of Turin, Italy. The rest of the world was uninterested in the relic. Historians and archaeologists had proven that hundreds of medieval relics were fakes, and most educated people assumed the shroud was also a forgery.

From May 25 to June 2 of 1898, the keepers of the shroud put it on public display to mark the Savoy family's fiftieth anniversary as rulers of Italy. To commemorate the occasion, King Umberto I of Italy asked a photographer named Secondo Pia to take the first photographs of the shroud.

Pia took several pictures, then went to his darkroom to develop the prints. Alone in the darkroom, the photographer gazed at the negatives of the shroud—and gasped. When viewed in negative—with dark spots light and light spots dark—the vague image on the shroud suddenly became detailed, three dimensional, and lifelike. Pia said later that he felt himself to be the first man in nineteen centuries to gaze on the true image of Jesus's body.

Secondo Pia's accidental discovery proved that the Shroud of Turin was a negative image, like an undeveloped photograph. This was amazing—and baffling—because viewers can only see such portrayals with the help of photography, a science developed in the 1800s. Why and how would someone make a medieval forgery with reversed properties of light?

Religious believers say the shroud is a true miracle. Scientists continue to puzzle over it. The negative imprint of the shroud is only one mysterious aspect among many that have fascinated and baffled scientists for more than a century.

GLOSSARY

camera obscura: A box or small darkened room into which an image of what is outside is projected using a small hole, and sometimes a simple lens, in one of the sides of the box or room.

organic: Characteristic of living things.

THE SHROUD IN SCRIPTURE

The Bible says nothing about a cloth imprinted with the image of Jesus's body. However, one book in the Bible, the Gospel according to John, does refer to Jesus's burial cloth. Chapter 19 of this Gospel relates how, after Jesus's death, Joseph of Arimathea and Nicodemus "took the body of Jesus and bound it in linen cloths" before burying it.

John chapter 20 tells that three days later, Mary Magdalene found Jesus's tomb empty and ran to tell the other disciples of her discovery. Simon Peter and "the other disciple, the one whom Jesus loved" ran to the empty tomb. There they found "the linen cloths lying, and the napkin, which had been on his head, not lying with the linen cloths but rolled up in a place by itself." In other words, Jesus's body was gone—but the cloths that had covered his body were still there.

How does this passage relate to the Shroud of Turin? First, the word translated "napkin" or "burial cloth" in modern Protestant Bible translations is the Greek word *sindon*, the technical term used to this day by the Catholic Church to describe the shroud. Allegedly, the Sindon in John's Gospel is the Shroud of Turin. This raises a question: Why does the Gospel not mention an image of Jesus imprinted on the Sindon? Such a miraculous image would only bolster belief in Jesus's resurrection—exactly the point this Gospel intended to make. Believers in the shroud suggest that perhaps the image had not yet formed on the shroud, or maybe the disciples were too excited to notice it at first. The shroud's miracle may have seemed far less amazing than the living presence of a man they had seen killed.

"The Shroud is a challenge to our intelligence."

—*Pope John Paul II, May 24, 1998*

THE SHROUD IN HISTORY

The first definite appearance of the shroud takes place in 1355. A French knight named Geoffrey de Charny displayed the shroud for the public in the tiny church of Lirey near Troyes. Charny was a financially poor knight and a previous Templar. The following year, Charny died at the Battle of Poiters, and the shroud's ownership passed to his infant son.

In 1389, Charny's son, Geoffrey de Charny II, placed the shroud back on display in the church at Lirey. The younger Charny claimed it was "the true Shroud of Jesus." The local bishop, Pierre d'Arcis, wrote to Pope Clement VII, telling him the shroud was a "cunningly painted" forgery. He demanded that the pope order Charny to stop displaying the shroud, but the Church leader denied the bishop's request.

Scholars have debated whether this exchange of letters in 1389 affects the shroud's authenticity. Skeptics point to the bishop's claim the shroud was "cunningly painted." Believers note the bishop had reason for jealousy: the little church at Lirey drew many worshippers away from larger and richer parishes.

What about the earlier history of the shroud? While 1355 is the earliest unmistakable reference to the relic, Australian historian Ian Wilson believes he can trace it much further back in time. The elder Charny was a Templar, and the Order of Knights Templar guarded the sacred relics in Jerusalem. When the Church persecuted the Templars, they and their relics went into hiding for a time. It is feasible that a French knight who had served in the Holy Land with the Templars could possess a relic such as the shroud.

The Templars were secretive, and separating fact from fiction regarding their history is not easy. Their opponents claimed the Templars worshipped a bearded head as if it were God. No one ever explained what this "head" was. Ian Wilson notes that in the past, the shroud was kept folded over eightfold. Folded thus, only the face of Christ—the most striking part of the shroud—was visible. Perhaps the Templars worshipped the face of Christ on the folded shroud.

For centuries before the Crusades, the Christian kingdom of Constantinople claimed ownership of a relic called the Edessa Cloth. Paintings of this Edessa Cloth resemble the face on the Shroud of Turin. According to ancient tradition, King Abgar V of Edessa converted to Christianity several decades after Jesus's death. The same tradition says a linen cloth imprinted with the image of Christ healed King Abgar of a deadly illness. The rulers of Constantinople kept this same cloth until the Crusaders took it in 1204. Thus, Ian Wilson claims to have traced the shroud from Charny to the Templar order, to Constantinople, to King Abgar, to Jesus Christ.

THE SHROUD & SCIENCE

Scientists have subjected the Shroud of Turin to more scientific testing than any other alleged holy relic. The more researchers learn about the shroud, the more it presents new mysteries.

In 1978, the Shroud of Turin Research Project (STURP) began. Twenty-four outstanding scientists from different countries, scientific backgrounds, and religious beliefs conducted an intense study of the shroud. Their research brought forth a number of fascinating results.

On March 24, the STURP team announced that the shroud was not a painting. The 1389 charge by French Bishop d'Arcis that the shroud was "cunningly painted" appears to be false. An American scientist, Dr. Walter McCrone, disagreed, however. McCrone became famous in 1973 for his pronouncement that a famous Viking map owned by Yale

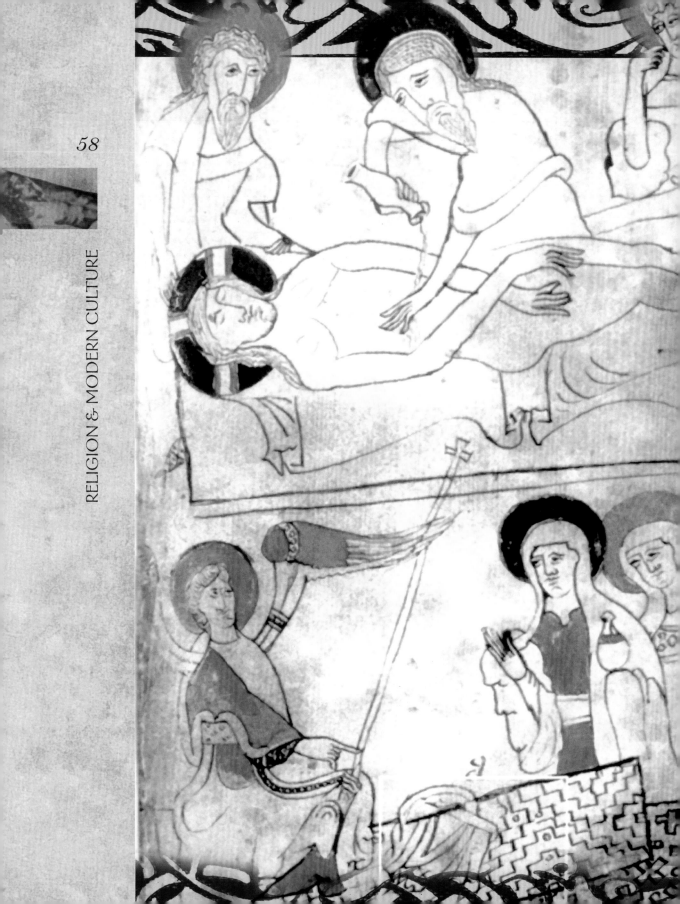

University was a modern forgery. In 1987, though, Crocker Laboratory of California reversed McCrone's verdict on the map, today, Yale University regards it as authentic. As of 2005, McCrone continued to write that the shroud is a painting. All other scientists who have seen the shroud and conducted analyses of its linen threads agree it is not a painting.

The STURP team made another amazing discovery regarding the shroud's photographic qualities. Dr. John Jackson, a coleader of the STURP team, brought in a VP-8 Image Analyzer, which had been recently developed by U.S. space scientists. The Image Analyzer takes a one-dimensional image and turns light and dark sections into three-dimensional heights. Artists' paintings lack any such three-dimensional qualities. To the scientists' astonishment, when they scanned the shroud with the VP-8 Analyzer, it produced a perfect three-dimensional image.

Medical doctors also studied the shroud, looking at the patterns of blood on the image. Numerous physicians have agreed that the blood marks on the Shroud of Turin man could only be produced by one method—an actual corpse, crucified as described in the New Testament, had to be placed on the linen. Doctors have also analyzed the blood. It is without doubt genuine human blood.

Historians and archaeologists have also examined the shroud. They note that the man portrayed on the shroud was crucified in genuine first-century Roman style. This is noteworthy because Europeans during the Middle Ages did not understand how the Romans actually performed crucifixions. People in medieval times assumed Roman executioners hammered nails through the victims' palms. All known artists' paintings of the crucifixion made during the Middle Ages picture the nails through Jesus's palms. This is not historically accurate, because the weight of a body would pull spikes right through the flesh of the hand. Instead, Roman executioners nailed their victims to the crossbeam through the wrist, since the bones there are strong enough to hold a body upright for an indefinite length of time. Archaeologists' findings

"He was pierced through for our faults,
Crushed for our sins,
On him lies the punishment that brings us peace,
And through his wounds we are healed."

—*words of the Hebrew prophet Isaiah, applied by Christians to the*
Crucifixion of Christ

verify this as the actual mode of ancient Roman crucifixion. The figure on the Shroud of Turin was undeniably nailed through the wrists—not through the palms.

The 1978 STURP project allowed experts in art, chemistry, photography, botany, textiles, history, and archaeology to study the shroud. They agreed it was not a painting. All evidence pointed to the shroud being the burial cloth for a first-century victim of crucifixion. Therefore, STURP team members were surprised and disappointed when a decade later other scientists pronounced the shroud a medieval forgery.

CARBON DATING & THE SHROUD

In 1983, King Umberto II of Italy died, and in his will, he gave the shroud to the Catholic Church. Five years later, the Vatican allowed scientists from Arizona, England, and Switzerland to do something almost unthinkable: cut off a little piece of the shroud for radiocarbon testing in their laboratories.

Scientists had been requesting this privilege for decades. Radiocarbon dating—also known as carbon-14 dating—can tell how old an **organic** object is based on the decay of its atomic matter. Scientists from the world's best radiocarbon laboratories dated their samples independently of each other. Then they conferred and announced their results to the world. They all agreed: the linen of the shroud was manufactured between 1260 and 1390. The Shroud of Turin was a forgery.

The result took STURP members by surprise. All their research had pointed to a first-century date for the shroud. Yet carbon-14 dating had proved accurate in innumerable cases. STURP members were disappointed, but they accepted the results. A few years later, however, two separate findings challenged the dating results.

Dr. Leoncio Garza-Valdes, known for his work on the blood of the shroud, is also a collector of Mayan jade artifacts. One of the pieces in his jade collection was carbon-14 tested and erroneously dated more than seven hundred years earlier than it actually was. Dr. Garza-Valdes knew this because of the artifact's artistic style. How could scientists be so wrong? Dr. Garza-Valdes determined that his jade artifact was covered with biomass; tiny bacteria were living on the surface of the object. Because these bacteria were alive, they skewed the results of the radiocarbon testing. The doctor then sought other examples of radiocarbon dating errors. He found cases where scientists dated Egyptian mummy wrappings a thousand years younger than the mummy itself. Obviously, this was impossible. He discovered that these mummy wrappings were also covered with biomass. When Dr. Garza-Valdes reexamined the shroud samples, he found biomass also coated their surfaces. He is convinced that this made the three laboratories more than a thousand years off in their dating of the shroud.

Raymond Rogers, a retired fellow of the Los Alamos National Laboratory who has some of the most impressive credentials of the scientists who have studied the shroud, disagrees with Garza-Valdes's bio-

mass theory. He studied similar samples and found no biomass. However, he too believes the carbon-14 dating of the shroud was incorrect.

In January of 2005, Dr. Rogers published an article in the scientific journal *Thermochimica Acta* titled "Studies on the Radiocarbon Sample from the Shroud of Turin." Rogers compared microscopic analysis of the samples taken from the shroud with samples from the main part of the shroud. Barrie Schwortz, a member of the STURP team and editor of the Shroud of Turin Web site, summarizes Rogers's article: "Rogers concluded that the radiocarbon sample is totally different in composition from the main part of the Shroud of Turin and was cut from a medieval reweaving of the cloth." In other words, holes in the shroud were patched during the Middle Ages, and this more recent fabric happened to be the sample used for the carbon-14 testing. This report, coming from a highly respected scientist and based on solid physical evidence, indicates that "the radiocarbon date was . . . not valid for determining the true age of the Shroud." A peer review by another chemist supports Rogers's claims.

THEORIES CONCERNING THE SHROUD

Despite intense research by dozens of top scientists, experts today are more mystified than ever by the Shroud of Turin. Science has proven what the shroud is *not*—it is not a medieval painting. Yet there is considerable disagreement concerning what the shroud is.

Several Christians have written books suggesting the shroud image formed when Jesus rose from the dead, emitting bursts of radiation from his resurrected body. The Gospels record an incident called the transfiguration, when the body of Jesus shone with blinding light. They believe a similar event occurred at the resurrection, producing the shroud image. However, Ray Rogers has examined the shroud fibers carefully and proven that no radioactive burst has ever hit the shroud.

Could some primitive form of camera have produced the image on the shroud? Professor Nicholas Allen, Dean of Art and Science at Technikon College, in Port Elizabeth, South Africa, has created a crude camera using only materials that existed in the fourteenth century. Professor Allen has used this camera to create an image on linen cloth that resembles that on the Shroud of Turin.

Allen's research proves the shroud could be a photograph. However, other researchers point out the unlikelihood of this being the case. Frenchman Joseph Nicephore Niepce produced the first known photograph in the year 1825. Projection devices known as *camera obscura* were used as far back as the fifth century BCE. However, as far as anyone knows, no one figured out how to transfer the projected image without painting it, until Niepce. It seems unlikely someone would single-handedly invent photography in the Middle Ages, use the technique to produce one object, and then disappear from history.

In 1997, authors Christopher Knight and Robert Lomas wrote a book titled *The Second Messiah: Templars, the Turin Shroud and the Great Secret of Freemasonry*. They suggest the shroud victim is not Jesus Christ, but the last leader of the Knights Templar, Jacques de Molay. Knight and Lomas believe that after de Molay's death, other knights wrapped his corpse in a shroud and an unusual chemical process produced the print. The shroud then became confused with that of Jesus Christ. The problem with this theory, according to historian Ian Wilson, is that no record exists of the crucifixion of de Molay. Furthermore, the shroud figure was crucified in ways that are authentic to first-century Roman crucifixion, methods yet unknown in the Middle Ages.

Ray Rogers has suggested a chemical process that could have created the shroud image. When bodies suffer physical trauma followed by death, they release high amounts of ammonia. If such chemicals were combined with the spices used to prepare burial wrappings in the first century, they could, over a long time span, produce the sort of faint

image seen on the shroud. Those who do believe the shroud is Jesus's burial cloth point out that this process works very slowly. Thus, at the time when the disciples entered the tomb as recounted in John's Gospel, the image would not yet have appeared on the cloth.

THE MEANING OF THE SHROUD

All the scientists and scholars who have studied the shroud agree it is a unique object. If it is a medieval forgery, then the person who manufactured the shroud was a genius. He had to learn how to crucify a man in a manner forgotten for more than a thousand years. Then he had to invent something like photography and produce a perfect negative image five centuries before anyone else did.

65

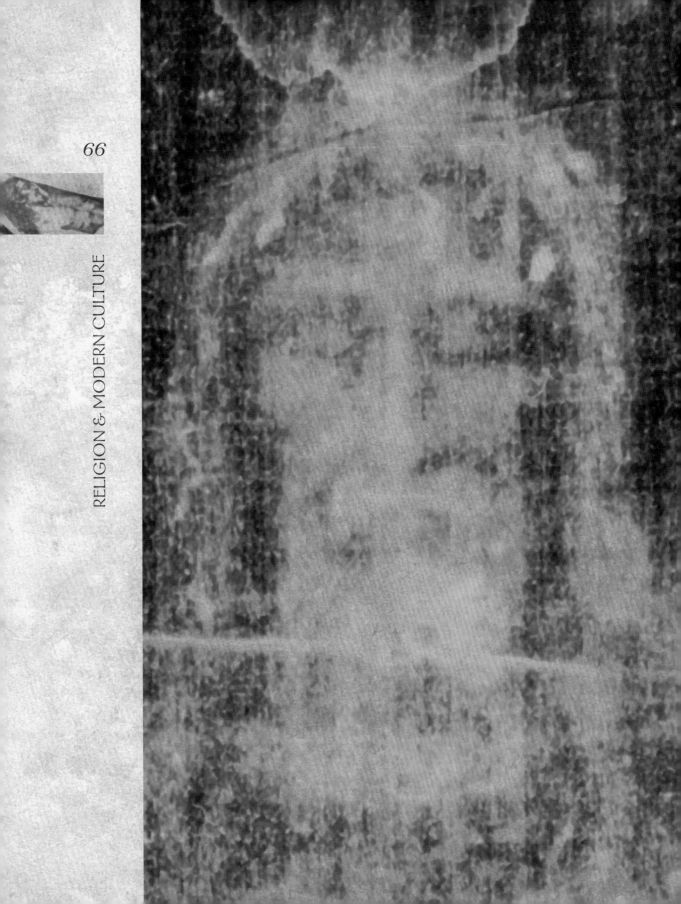

More likely, according to many experts, the shroud is an authentic artifact from the first century. Roman soldiers crucified a man. Later, someone placed his body in a linen cloth. Perhaps an unusual chemical process transferred the victim's image onto the shroud.

Was this victim of crucifixion Jesus Christ? Scientists who have spent decades studying the shroud say there is no way to know. Science can prove dates, analyze blood, and identify cause of death—yet there is no scientific test for "Jesus-ness." Rome crucified thousands of criminals and rebels in the first century. Theoretically, the man in the shroud could be any one of those victims.

At the same time, the shroud is an object of reverence for many Christians. If you have seen the movie *The Passion of the Christ*, you can get a sense of how important Christ's suffering is to Christian believers. Like that movie, the Shroud of Turin tells the story of Jesus's death for those who believe in him.

The Shroud of Turin is unique among relics. The physical object itself challenges scientists and theologians with its unusual properties. In contrast to the Shroud, the Holy Grail exists primarily in the realm of mythology. Lacking physical form, the Grail nonetheless holds a powerful grip on the minds of men and women. Outside of the Bible, it is the most influential myth in the Western world.

Chapter 5

ANCIENT LEGENDS OF THE HOLY GRAIL

Three men and a woman stand in an ancient grotto. Flickering candles illuminate the stone chamber. On a shelf before them are rows of ancient cups, some gold, others silver, all glittering in the candlelight. The woman is Professor Elsa Schneider. Her loyalties are dubious—sometimes she cooperates with the Nazis, sometimes with the good guys—but she is determined to possess the Holy Grail. One of the men is Walter Donavan. Like Schneider, Donavan will work for anyone—even Hitler—to get his hands on the Holy Grail. Professor Indiana Jones also stands in the cave, wearing his famous felt hat and leather jacket. Indiana has a more personal interest in the Holy Grail. His father is dying. If Indiana can quickly recover the Grail, then the magical goblet can restore his father's life.

Finally, there is the Grail Knight. Clad in **chain mail**, he has guarded the Grail for nine hundred years, kept miraculously alive by its mystical powers.

The Grail Knight tells his visitors, "You must choose wisely, for while the true Grail will bring you life, the false Grail will take it from you." Elsa scrutinizes the cups, then hands one to Donavan, who smiles. "Ah, yes." He closes his eyes and drinks from the cup. Then he begins to shake. Fear seizes the occupants of the cave. Donavan's eyes pop out, his skin melts, and he catches on fire. Dr. Schneider screams as Donavan dissolves into a pile of ashes.

As Jones and Schneider recover from their horror, the Grail Knight calmly remarks, "He did not choose wisely."

THE HOLY GRAIL

The movie *Indiana Jones and the Last Crusade* is just one version of the myth of the Holy Grail, a myth being a story expressing truths that give its hearers meaning for life. The Holy Grail is one of the most important myths of Western civilization. From the twelfth century until today, the Grail myth has been retold countless times. In each age, men and women have interpreted the Holy Grail in ways that fulfill their own longings.

The Holy Grail, in all of its tellings, is one object. However, the Grail takes many different forms in various versions of the story. In the classical accounts, it is most often the cup from which Jesus drank at the Last Supper. That same cup, according to the Grail myth, was used to catch Christ's blood as he died on the cross. In other classical versions, the Grail is a magical dish, a miraculous stone, or a secret book. More recently, New-Agers and a popular novelist have interpreted the Grail as a living woman, the physical descendant of Jesus Christ. In each of its

GLOSSARY

chain mail: Interlinked metal rings that make a flexible piece of armor worn by medieval knights.

venerated: Honored something or somebody as sacred or special.

various forms, the Grail is more than the physical object itself. It represents fulfillment, self-realization, or an encounter with God or the Goddess.

To understand this ever-changing and always-popular myth, we must trace its roots. The Grail myth first appeared in the Middle Ages. In medieval times, the myth was influenced by three different traditions: Celtic (pagan) legend, Christian doctrine, and alchemy.

THE GRAIL & CELTIC (PAGAN) LEGENDS

The French author Chrétien de Troyes wrote the first account of the Grail. In 1181, he published *La Conte du Graal* (*The Story of the Grail*), which tells the story of Perceval, one of King Arthur's knights. Perceval, raised by his mother in a forest, away from other people, is simple and

"The Grail of romances is not to be found in cathedral treasuries or among the possessions of the great monasteries. It is too holy an object for this sinful world."

—*Richard Barber, noted medieval historian*

innocent. One day, he meets knights in armor in his woods. The knights fascinate Perceval, and he decides to leave his mother and journey to Camelot, where he will become a knight. The country boy has no manners or knowledge of the world, so he makes countless social blunders and several times hurts other people due to his ignorance.

The center of the story is Perceval's visit to the Fisher King's castle in the midst of a wasteland. The entire kingdom suffers because the Fisher King has a wound in his genitals. The wound will not heal, but the Holy Grail keeps the king alive.

At the Fisher King's castle, Perceval sees the Grail while a maiden, "fair and comely and beautifully adorned," carries it. "When she entered holding the Grail, so brilliant a light appeared that the candles lost their brightness like the stars or the moon when the sun rises." In this story, the Grail is a magical platter that the Grail Maiden places before each guest at the table. As she does so, the Grail magically fills with whatever delicious food each guest desires. Thus, in its first appearance, the Grail is a cornucopia—a vessel that magically produces endless amounts of food. It also has the power to heal deadly wounds.

Chrétien de Troyes does not present the Grail as most people think of it today. It is not the *Holy* Grail, the cup of Jesus Christ. Instead, the Grail is a plate that magically serves its owner. Where did he get this story?

The word "grail" (*graal* in French) means "bowl, plate, or goblet." A grail could be any vessel used to serve food or drink.

Historians agree de Troyes wrote down what storytellers had passed by word of mouth from the ancient Celts. The Celts were formidable warriors living in Europe and Britain from the time of ancient Rome through the Middle Ages. Prior to their acceptance of Christianity, the Celts worshipped various gods and goddesses who inhabited the forces of nature. According to the pagan Celts, a mythical hero named Bran owned a magical cauldron that provided endless amounts of food to Bran's warriors. The Celtic legend of Bran inspired Chrétien de Troyes' novel about the Grail.

Another version of the Grail story may be as old as de Troyes' *La Conte du Graal.* The story of *Peredur,* written in the region of Wales, is similar to that of Perceval; both legends obviously have the same hero. However, the Welsh myth contains the most macabre version of the Grail. In *Peredur,* the Grail is a platter that holds a severed head that tells fortunes. Once again, the Grail is a relic from Celtic myth. According to ancient Celtic legend, after Bran was killed, his head continued to live—and tell fortunes—for many decades.

Scholars who study ancient legends see the roots of the Grail myth in pre-Christian Celtic traditions. However, the dominant force in medieval Europe was the Church. Christian writers soon took the myth of the Grail and made it their own.

THE GODDESS & THE GRAIL

Celtic goddesses also play important roles in the myth of the Holy Grail. In *La Conte du Graal*, the Grail Maiden is a woman of great beauty who always accompanies the Grail. Another woman, a hideous hag, magically appears at points in the story to guide Perceval. The legend of Perceval is part of a larger series of stories—the legends of King Arthur. A casual reader might think Arthurian myths are male stories; they tell of various knights hacking and spearing one another. However, powerful, mysterious, and magical women control these warriors.

For example, King Arthur receives his invincible sword, Excalibur, from the Lady of the Lake. In pagan Celtic myth, local goddesses protect lakes and ponds. Celtic nobles would cast special weapons into the lakes as offerings to the goddess of the lake. Morgan La Fay, Arthur's half sister, is a mighty sorceress who overcomes the great magician Merlin and ultimately ends Camelot. Scholars agree Morgan is the Celtic goddess Modron. Medieval writers sometimes refer to her as "Morgan the goddess."

CHRISTIAN GRAIL MYTHS

The night before Roman soldiers arrested and killed him, Jesus of Nazareth celebrated the Jewish Pesach meal with his closest companions. He took a cup of wine and said, "This is my blood, the new covenant, which is poured out for the forgiveness of sins." Doing this, he attached symbolic meaning to the cup. The wine represented his sacrificial death. Christians believe that Christ's death is the means by which they draw close to God the Creator, and by doing so receive wholeness, forgiveness, and love. Thus, the cup used in a Holy Communion ceremony is a powerful symbol representing all the blessings that Jesus brings to Christian believers. In the words of an old Christian hymn, "There is power, power, wonder-working power in the precious blood" of Jesus Christ.

At the beginning of the thirteenth century, leaders of the Catholic Church emphasized the doctrine of transubstantiation. This theological term means that the cup of wine when served in a communion ceremony actually changes from wine to the physical blood of Jesus Christ. For faithful Catholics, the Mass became a truly miraculous event.

Beginning around the year 800, portrayals of Jesus's Crucifixion include a figure standing beneath the cross collecting the blood of Christ in a cup. In some pictures, Joseph of Arimathea collects the blood. (Joseph was the rich man who, according to Christian tradition, provided his tomb for Jesus's burial.) In other pictures, Jesus's mother, Mary, holds the cup into which Christ's blood falls.

At the end of the eighth century, another French writer, Robert de Boron, wrote *L'Estoire dou Graal* (*The History of the Grail*). De Boron Christianized the Grail, giving the cup its most famous form, and the Grail now became the *Holy* Grail. According to de Boron, Jesus drank from this very cup at the Last Supper. Furthermore, Joseph of Arimathea took that cup and collected the blood that dripped from

Jesus's side as he hung on the cross. Afterward, Joseph took the cup to England. Centuries later, King Arthur and his band of Christian knights needed to find the cup in order to heal the land.

This new Grail myth became widely popular. Hundreds of authors wrote Christian versions of the Grail myth in Latin, French, and English. Wandering troubadours sang songs about the Grail in knightly courts. This version of the legend fit perfectly with the needs of medieval society. It encouraged the teaching of the Church regarding the Mass, and it gave Europe a role in sacred history. Despite its Celtic pagan roots, the Grail had become Christian.

"The Grail was bliss's fruit, such sufficiency of this world's sweetness that it almost counterweighed what is spoken of the Heavenly Kingdom."

    —*from* Parsival

"PARZIVAL"—THE GRAIL MYTH TAKES ANOTHER TWIST

Wolfram Von Eschenbach was a German poet and teller of tall tales. We might compare Von Eschenbach's stories to the *X-Files* of our own age. He loved things that were strange, mysterious, and rumored to be true. Von Eschenbach was especially interested in alchemy, the medieval science that combined magical superstition with the beginnings of chemistry. He was also intrigued by astrology and by the knowledge and beliefs of the Muslim world.

Parzival is Von Eschenbach's version of the Perceval story—but with all sorts of odd additions. In *Parzival*, the Grail is a large stone. Von Eschenbach calls the Grail stone by the Latin name *lapsit exillis*. Students of medieval Latin have puzzled without satisfaction over the meaning of the words. The lapsit exillis keeps those who stay near it eternally youthful in appearance.

Parzival introduces another new element to the Grail story, the Fellowship of the Grail. This is an order of holy knights and ladies who throughout all generations guard the stone. *Parzival* refers to the Fellowship of the Grail with the German word Templeisen. Some scholars say the word refers to the Knights Templar. However, Templars did not marry; they were monks who swore never to have sex. In *Parzival*, the Fellowship of the Grail members are men and women who marry and have children.

Von Eschenbach's version of the Grail myth was not very popular in the Middle Ages, but it has been influential since then. *Parzival* provides several important elements found in *Indiana Jones and the Last Crusade*.

On the darker side, Von Eschenbach's *Parzival* fascinated an angry young man in 1920s Berlin. When Adolf Hitler read the fantasy, it led to the dictator's quest for the Holy Grail during World War II.

TANGIBLE GRAILS

The Middle Ages' desire for actual, physical relics inspired medieval artisans to produce many alleged "Holy Grail" objects. The green glass *Sacro Catino* (Holy Bowl), now in the Museum of the Cathedral of San Lorenzo, Genoa, Spain, is one such alleged holy relic. Another is the *Santo Caliz* (Holy Chalice) in the cathedral of Valencia, Spain. The Roman Catholic Church declared the Santo Caliz a holy relic, and Pope John Paul II once used it for a special Mass. Visitors to New York City can stop in at the Metropolitan Museum of Art and gaze at the *Antioch Chalice*, another Grail candidate Orthodox Christians have **venerated** since at least the sixth century. For centuries, monks have guarded the *Nanteos Cup*, a simple wooden mug from a church in Wales, as being the Grail. More recently, British author Graham Philips has championed an ancient alabaster jar found in a collector's home in Britain as being "the Chalice of Magdalene, the cup that held the blood of Christ."

None of these alleged Holy Grails get a thumbs-up from archaeologists. Most were manufactured during the Middle Ages. Even those that are more ancient cannot be proven to be the cup used by Christ. The best place to look for the Holy Grail is in the meanings of the legends that surround it.

Ultimately, the Grail myths show us what people believed about their world at certain points in history. For Celtic warriors during the Dark Ages, the Grail was a magical plate. It provided food, told fortunes, and allowed them to communicate with the goddesses who controlled their fates. In later medieval times, it was the cup of Jesus Christ.

It held the blood of Christ that brought salvation, the same blood celebrated in the Mass. For Wolfram Von Eschenbach, it was a mystical stone like those used by alchemists. With all these variations, the Grail myth was just beginning. Today, the Holy Grail has again gained control of hearts and minds, this time due to a popular novel.

Chapter 6

A MODERN GRAIL MYTH

Harvard professor Robert Langdon and French code expert Sophie Neveu have escaped from the French police and from an albino assassin sent by Opus Dei, the Catholic religious order. They have been to the Louvre Museum and the Swiss National Bank picking up clues to the greatest secret of all time. Now, they visit with Sir Leigh Teabing, an authority on the Holy Grail. Teabing is about to reveal the true secret of the Holy Grail.

"*The Holy Grail is Mary Magdalene . . . the mother of the royal blood line of Jesus Christ.*" Teabing explains that ancient Christian documents called the Gnostic Gospels tell of Jesus's marriage to Mary Magdalene. Jesus and Mary had a child, and through the centuries, secret societies have guarded Jesus's descendants. Teabing claims the Christian church has hidden and suppressed this truth. A secret society, the Priory of Sion, founded in 1099, passes down this hidden knowledge. Leonardo da Vinci was a member of the Priory and revealed clues in his paintings.

These "secrets" are no secret to the millions who have read Dan Brown's *The Da Vinci Code,* from which the story above is taken. Thanks to this best-selling novel, the bloodline of Jesus Christ and Mary Magdalene has become the Holy Grail myth for the twenty-first century. Many readers realize, "It is just a novel," yet numerous fans of *The Da Vinci Code* wonder if it might be more than mere fiction. Dan Brown himself states on the first page of the book, "All descriptions of artwork, architecture, documents and secret rituals in this novel are accurate."

Paul L. Maier, professor of ancient history at Western Michigan University, asks, "Can you identify even *one* serious scholar, writer, professional authority, historian or theologian anywhere in the world who agrees with Brown?" According to Dr. Maier, scholarly support for *The Da Vinci Code* is altogether lacking.

HISTORY & "THE DA VINCI CODE"

The main source of information for *The Da Vinci Code* is the "nonfiction" best seller *Holy Blood, Holy Grail,* published in 1982 by authors Michael Baigent, Richard Leigh, and Henry Lincoln. *The Da Vinci Code* follows that book so closely that Michael Baigent and Richard Leigh sued Random House, publisher of *The Da Vinci Code,* in March of 2004, claiming that Dan Brown plagiarized their work. Richard Leigh told the

GLOSSARY

celibate: A person who abstains from sex, especially because of a religious vow.

conservative: Resistant to change.

feminist theology: A movement to reconsider the traditions, practices, scriptures, and theologies of Western religions from a feminist perspective.

fundamentalist: Follower of a religious or political movement based on a literal interpretation of and strict adherence to a doctrine.

British *Telegraph* newspaper, "It's not that Dan Brown has lifted certain ideas because a number of people have done that before. It's rather that he's lifted the whole architecture—the whole jigsaw puzzle—and hung it onto the peg of a fictional thriller."

Dan Brown's novel is escapist fiction, not carefully thought-out history or theology. Critics point to the fact that the book isn't even particularly well written. And yet *The Da Vinci Code* has tapped into the modern world's hunger for myth.

*"The quest for the Holy Grail is the quest to kneel
before the bones of Mary Magdalene."*
—The Da Vinci Code

THE FOUNDATION FOR "THE DA VINCI CODE"

The Da Vinci Code asserts that the Gnostic Gospels reveal Jesus's marriage to Mary Magdalene. The Gnostic Gospels are real. An Arab peasant named Muhammad Ali found them while searching for fertilizer in 1945 near the town of Nag Hammadi Egypt. (You can read all the Gnostic Gospels in the book *The Nag Hammadi Library* by James M. Robinson.)

Dan Brown quotes the Gospel of Philip as evidence of Jesus's marriage to Magdalene. The Gospel of Philip says of Mary Magdalene that Jesus "loved her more than all the disciples and used to kiss her often on her [word missing in the original]." James Robinson is general editor of the *Nag Hammadi Library*. When *U.S. News & World Report* interviewed him for *Secrets of* The Da Vinci Code, they asked if the kiss in the Gospel of Philip implied marriage between Jesus and Magdalene. Robinson replied, "The writer of the Gospel of Philip clearly disdains physical sex as beastly. And too much has been made of this kiss. There is another Nag Hammadi text in which Jesus kisses James on the mouth. Does that make him homosexual?"

Gnostic texts are filled with symbolic meanings. The "kiss on the lips" in Gnostic terms was an expression for spiritual illumination. These ancient documents do portray Mary Magdalene as an especially spiritual follower of Jesus—but not as his sex partner.

Elaine Pagels, a Princeton professor and authority on the Gnostics, is certainly no *fundamentalist* and is willing to disagree with traditional Christian beliefs. When asked her view on the Jesus–Mary

"As for Dan Brown's fanciful conspiracy theory about the Church's cover-up of a Magdalene–Jesus union, it is almost beyond comprehension that a tale so rooted in demonstrable falsehoods could be so quickly and easily embraced by the public."

—*Richard Abanes, nationally recognized authority on cults and religions, in his book* The Truth Behind *The Da Vinci Code.*

Magdalene sexual union, Pagels says, "The weight of evidence that we have suggests to me the contrary, that in fact he was a **celibate**."

What about the "hidden meanings" in Leonardo da Vinci's paintings? Serious scholars of Leonardo's deny that *The Last Supper* portrays Mary Magdalene. Diane Apostolos-Cappadona, adjunct professor of religious art and cultural history at Georgetown University, says the idea of a woman in *The Last Supper* "fits nicely with **feminist theology**. However that doesn't make it true." She explains that the figure next to Christ is the Apostle John, and "There is a tradition of John being seen in our eyes as soft, feminine and youthful." In fact, Apostolos-Cappadona points out that the gender of many figures in Renaissance paintings is difficult to distinguish.

The most important part of *The Da Vinci Code*'s claims is a secret organization called the Priory of Sion. According to Brown's mythology, the Priory is a real secret organization, more than a thousand years old, which for centuries has guarded the bloodline of Christ and Magdalene. However, what Dan Brown says on page one is "fact" is pure fiction. An article by French scholar Amy Bernstein titled "The French Confection" reveals the facts regarding the Priory of Sion. The Priory of Sion, which Brown claims originated in 1099, actually dates only to 1956. It was the invention of one man—Pierre Plantard. Plantard was unemployed at

A PHYSICAL CONNECTION WITH JESUS?

In November of 2002, the magazine *Biblical Archaeology Review* published one of the most exciting headlines in the history of the magazine: "World Exclusive: Evidence of Jesus Written in Stone." The article explained, "Amazing as it may sound, a limestone bone box (called an 'ossuary') has surfaced in Israel that may once have contained the bones of James, the brother of Jesus." It went on to explain that this ossuary had an inscription on the side, written in ancient Aramaic script: "James, son of Joseph, brother of Jesus."

The discovery seemed too good to be true; it was almost like finding the Holy Grail. In fact, it *was* too good to be true. Experts soon voiced concern that the writing might be forged. In 2004, the Israeli government arrested the owner of the ossuary, Oded Golan, for manufacturing fake biblical objects. The incident was disappointing to many Christian believers, yet it again revealed the public desire for biblical relics.

the time and, according to Bernstein, already "served four months in Fresnes prison . . . convicted of fraud and embezzlement." Bernstein says a number of respected French researchers have established that, "At the beginning of the 1960s, Plantard launched a concerted effort to forge a trail of documentation . . . to establish . . . the Priory of Sion." In other words, the organization that is the most important part of *The Da Vinci Code* is a modern-day hoax.

THE POWER OF A MODERN GRAIL MYTH

What is the secret behind *The Da Vinci Code's* success? In a way, the latest Grail myth is similar to the medieval ones; it has little to do with historical facts, yet it provides meaning in a way that speaks powerfully to the culture.

Dan Brown's *The Da Vinci Code* fits well with today's spiritual mindset. Surveys show that U.S. citizens are interested in spirituality, and many desire to form their own individual beliefs about religious matters. *The Da Vinci Code* offers a spiritual view of the world. It ties into ancient religious images that many readers recall from their growing up years. Yet it completely changes these ancient images, making them fresh and intriguing.

Furthermore, *The Da Vinci Code* portrays organized religion—in particular the Catholic Church—as untrustworthy. That suits many North American readers who likewise distrust religious institutions. Especially in Canada, but also in the United States, church attendance of younger people is dropping. Around the same time that *The Da Vinci Code* came out, media reports further eroded public confidence by exposing the Catholic Church's protection of priests who had molested children. For the past thirty years or more, a majority of North American Catholics have disagreed with the Church's teachings regarding birth

95

RELIGION & MODERN CULTURE

control, abortion, and women's exclusion from the priesthood. Large numbers of religious people in the twenty-first century do not believe in the restrictions conservative religion places on sexual behavior. In such a climate, many readers find comfort in the idea that Jesus experienced a sexual life—contrary to the traditions of the churches.

Finally, and perhaps most important, *The Da Vinci Code* fits a need expressed by many spiritual seekers today—the need for an image of the Divine Feminine. Many Christian churches have historically downplayed women's roles in religion. Some **conservative** Protestant churches do not allow women to lead or teach in religious services. Through the ages, theologians have most often portrayed God as male. Many religious women and men desire a faith that portrays female figures as worthy of worship. Worship of the Goddess is growing rapidly, though it is still small in proportion to Christianity, Judaism, and Islam. Within Christianity and Judaism, many teachers and laypeople are discovering feminine images of deity in their scriptures. Brown acknowledges his indebtedness to New-Age religionist Margaret Starbird, author of *Goddess in the Gospels. The Da Vinci Code* is the first novel to give prominence to the Goddess, and doing so, it taps into a significant spiritual yearning.

THE INNER QUEST

Jack Lucas is a radio shock jock akin to Howard Stern. He insults and upsets his listeners—and is famous for doing so. One night, Lucas's radio act goes hellishly off course. Inspired by the shock jock's comments, a listener goes to a disco and guns down the dancers before killing himself. Overwhelmed with guilt, Lucas drops out of society. He lives with his girlfriend, yet he cannot express any genuine emotion.

One night, as Lucas is considering suicide, he meets a homeless man named Parry who is obsessed with the Holy Grail. Parry believes he is a sort of modern-day knight on the Grail quest. Lucas discovers that Parry has not always been homeless. He used to be a successful businessman, until his wife was gunned down in the bar incident that Lucas inspired.

> *"Such power does the stone bestow upon man that his flesh and bones immediately acquire youth. That stone is . . . the Grail."*
>
> —*from* Parzival *by Wolfram Von Eschenbach*

Lucas decides to try and help Parry resume a "normal" life. Yet Parry, even with his delusions, is happier and healthier than Lucas is. One night, as the two men lie on the grass in Central Park, Parry shares a story with Lucas:

It begins with the king as a boy, having to spend the night alone in the forest to prove his courage so he can become king. Now while he is spending the night alone, he's visited by a sacred vision. Out of the fire appears the Holy Grail, symbol of God's divine grace. A voice said to the boy, "You shall be keeper of the Grail so that it may heal the hearts of men." But the boy was blinded by greater visions of a life filled with power and glory and beauty. And in this state of radical amazement he felt for a brief moment not like a boy, but invincible, like God, . . . so he reached into the fire to take the Grail, . . . and the Grail vanished, . . . leaving him with his hand in the fire to be terribly wounded.

Now as this boy grew older, his wound grew deeper. Until one day, life for him lost its reason. . . . He had no faith in any man, not even himself. . . . He couldn't love or feel loved. . . . He was sick with experience. He began to die.

GLOSSARY

epiphany: The appearance of a divine being.

One day a fool wandered into the castle and found the king alone. And being a fool, he was simple minded, he didn't see a king. He only saw a man alone and in pain. And he asked the king, "What ails you friend?" The king replied, "I'm thirsty. I need some water to cool my throat." So the fool took a cup from beside his bed, filled it with water and handed it to the king. As the king began to drink, he realized his wound was healed. He looked in his hands and there was the Holy Grail, that which he sought all of his life. And he turned to the fool and said with amazement, "How can you find that which my brightest and bravest could not?" And the fool replied, "I don't know. I only knew that you were thirsty." (from *The Fisher King* by Richard LaGravenese)

This story allows the former radio personality to begin to live again. A homeless man has given him illumination, and the Grail begins its healing work. All this takes place in Terry Gilliam's 1991 film *The Fisher King*, starring Jeff Bridges and Robin Williams, a brilliant film that's touching, spiritual, and gritty at the same time.

"The search for the Grail is the search for the divine in all of us."

—*Marcus Brody, in* Indiana Jones and the Last Crusade

The Fisher King reminds us of the true nature of the Holy Grail. The Grail as a physical object has always been less important than the story about how the hero must journey to find the Grail. In his travels, the hero grows spiritually. Whether in ancient Celtic myths or the modern myth of *The Da Vinci Code*, the quest for the Grail is primarily an inner, spiritual quest.

One goal of the quest for the Holy Grail is healing. In the very first Grail story, *La Conte Du Graal*, an entire kingdom suffers along with the Fisher King. If Perceval (the fool) completes his quest for the Grail, the whole land will heal.

Likewise, in *Indiana Jones and the Last Crusade*, Indiana must retrieve the Grail to save his wounded father. At the end of the movie, the father and son have experienced more than physical healing. For years, Indiana and his father have been angry with one another, but at the movie's end, they have reconciled. In his last scene, Henry Jones (the father) says he has found "illumination." The quest is accomplished. The Grail has brought wisdom and healing.

Margaret Starbird, in her book *The Goddess in the Gospels*, speaks of the importance of her beliefs and asserts that Mary Magdalene, "the lost Bride of Jesus," is "the lost Grail." She says that when the lost Grail is again recognized by the world, it will "heal our . . . relationships and our personal woundedness, making us joyful, making us whole!"

A HILARIOUS GRAIL QUEST

In every version, the quest for the Holy Grail is a myth with profound spiritual insights . . . well, except for one version: *Monty Python and the Holy Grail* is pure comedy. There is hardly a moment in the film free from inspired zaniness. From the first moment, when King Arthur appears galloping without a horse, followed by a servant clapping coconuts together, to the final insane scenes with the killer rabbit and holy hand grenade, audiences chuckle and howl with laughter. If laughter really is the best medicine, then perhaps *Monty Python and the Holy Grail* is another form of the Grail's healing work.

The healing power of the Holy Grail in *The Fisher King*, *The Last Crusade*, and *The Goddess in the Gospels* reminds us, again, of the power of myth. Believers invest holy objects with power. Whereas Hitler sought the Spear of Destiny for selfish and destructive reasons, others have sought the Grail for healing. Perhaps relics function as mirrors: they bring out what is inside a person—evil or good.

THE QUEST FOR DIVINE ENCOUNTER

In a medieval painting, the Knights of the Round Table are seated around the Holy Grail. From the inside of the cup, Jesus himself rises up, with arms uplifted to bless the knights. As quaint as this image may seem today, it was deeply meaningful for medieval Christians. The quest for the Holy Grail was ultimately the quest for contact with God himself (or herself). When the Grail appears, it is an *epiphany*, a direct experience of the Divine presence. Likewise, the modern Grail myth ends with an epiphany. At the very end of *The Da Vinci Code*, Dan Brown relates that, "with a sudden upwelling of reverence, Robert Langdon fell to his knees," paying homage to the Goddess.

Over the ages, every version of the Grail quest has concluded in the posture of worship. The object of worship varies—it may be an ancient Celtic nature deity, or Jesus Christ, or the Goddess Mary Magdalene, but an encounter with the Grail is also an experience of the Divine Presence.

The fourth-century theologian Saint Augustine once said, "Thou hast made us for thyself, O Lord; and our heart is restless until it rests in thee." Perhaps that is the heart of the Grail myth's timeless fascination: human beings' universal sense of yearning for the Divine.

FURTHER READING

Abanes, Richard. *The Truth Behind* The Da Vinci Code. Eugene, Ore.: Harvest House, 2004.

Barber, Richard. *The Holy Grail: Imagination and Belief.* Cambridge, Mass.: Harvard University Press, 2004.

Brown, Dan. *The Da Vinci Code.* New York: Doubleday, 2003.

Bulfinch, Thomas. *Bulfinch's Age of Chivalry or King Arthur and His Knights.* Mineola, N.Y.: Dover, 2004.

Cox, Simon. *Cracking* The Da Vinci Code: *The Unauthorized Guide to the Facts Behind Dan Brown's Bestselling Novel.* New York: Barnes & Noble, 2004.

Godwin, Malcolm. *The Holy Grail: Its Origins, Secrets & Meaning Revealed.* New York: Barnes & Noble, 1998.

Griffin, Justin E. *The Holy Grail: The Legend, the History, the Evidence.* Jefferson, N.C.: McFarland, 2001.

Hancock, Graham. *The Sign and the Seal.* New York: Simon & Schuster, 1992.

Robinson, James M. *The Nag Hammadi Library.* San Francisco: Harper, 1990.

Schwortz, Barrie, and Ian Wilson. *The Turin Shroud: The Illustrated Evidence.* New York: Barnes & Noble, 2000.

FOR MORE INFORMATION

An Introduction to Current
Theories about the Holy Grail
www.byu.edu/ipt/projects/
middleages/Arthur/Grail.html

Frequently Asked Questions
About the Shroud of Turin
(by Ray Rogers, chemist and
leader of the STURP team)
www.shroud.com/pdfs/
rogers5faqs.pdf

The Holy Shroud—
Official Turin Site
sindone.torino.chiesacattolica.it/
en/welcome.htm

King Arthur and the Holy Grail
www.greatdreams.com/
arthur.html

Mary Magdalene
www.newadvent.org/cathen/
09761a.htm

The Shroud of Turin Web site
(by noted authority on the Shroud
Barrie Schwortz)
www.shroud.com

The Shroud of Turin
Education Project
www.shroud2000.com/
LatestNews-Menu.htm

Spear of Destiny
ourworld.cs.com/argentprime/
spear.htm

The Official Graham Phillips
Web site—the Search for the Grail
homepage.ntlworld.com/
yvan.cartwright/Books/Grail.htm

World History.com—the Holy Grail
www.worldhistory.com/wiki/H/
Holy-Grail.htm

Publisher's note:
The Web sites listed on this page were active at the time of publication.
The publisher is not responsible for Web sites that have changed their
addresses or discontinued operation since the date of publication. The
publisher will review and update the Web-site list upon each reprint.

PICTURE CREDITS

The illustrations in RELIGION AND MODERN CULTURE are photo montages made by Dianne Hodack. They are a combination of her original mixed-media paintings and collages, the photography of Benjamin Stewart, various historical public-domain artwork, and other royalty-free photography collections.

AUTHOR: Kenneth McIntosh is a freelance writer living in Flagstaff Arizona. He lives with his wife, Marsha, and has two children, Jonathan and Eirené. He has a bachelor's degree in English and a master's degree in theology. He is the author of more than a dozen books. He formerly spent a decade teaching junior high in inner-city Los Angeles, and another decade serving as an ordained minister. He enjoys hiking, boogie boarding, and vintage Volkswagens.

CONSULTANT: Dr. Marcus J. Borg is the Hundere Distinguished Professor of Religion and Culture in the Philosophy Department at Oregon State University. Dr. Borg is past president of the Anglican Association of Biblical Scholars. Internationally known as a biblical and Jesus scholar, the *New York Times* called him "a leading figure among this generation of Jesus scholars." He is the author of twelve books, which have been translated into eight languages. Among them are *The Heart of Christianity: Rediscovering a Life of Faith* (2003) and *Meeting Jesus Again for the First Time* (1994), the best-selling book by a contemporary Jesus scholar.

CONSULTANT: Dr. Robert K. Johnston is Professor of Theology and Culture at Fuller Theological Seminary in Pasadena, California, having served previously as Provost of North Park University and as a faculty member of Western Kentucky University. The author or editor of thirteen books and twenty-five book chapters (including *The Christian at Play*, 1983; *The Variety of American Evangelicalism*, 1991; *Reel Spirituality: Theology and Film in Dialogue*, 2000; *Life Is Not Work/Work Is Not Life: Simple Reminders for Finding Balance in a 24/7 World*, 2000; *Finding God in the Movies: 33 Films of Reel Faith*, 2004; and *Useless Beauty: Ecclesiastes Through the Lens of Contemporary Film*, 2004), Johnston is the immediate past president of the American Theological Society, an ordained Protestant minister, and an avid bodysurfer.